STORIES

OSCAR MÉTÉNIER (1859–1913), the son of a *commissaire de police*, was a French playwright and novelist. In 1897 he founded the Grand-Guignol theater in Paris, which became renowned for its shocking stage presentations. His works include the novel *Zézette* (1891), the one-act play *Lui!* (1897), and the novel *Curaçao-Roi* which he collaborated on with Delphi Fabrice.

DANIEL CORRICK is an editor and literary historian with a specialist interest in nineteenth-century literature, especially the evolution of Gothicism and the Decadent movement. He has worked on a number of volumes including the collected fiction of Montague Summers, and unpublished works of Edgar Saltus and Edward Heron-Allen. In addition, he has edited several anthologies, including *Sorcery and Sanctity: A Homage to Arthur Machen* (Hieroglyphic Press, 2013), and *Drowning in Beauty: The Neo-Decadent Anthology* (Snuggly Books, 2018).

OSCAR MÉTÉNIER

THREE DECADENT STORIES

translated by Daniel Corrick

THIS IS A SNUGGLY BOOK

ISBN: 978-1-64525-147-7

CONTENTS

THREE DECADENT STORIES

THE LIZARD

AT the Buttes-Chaumont. Laying in the shadow of a great boulder, with his belly in the air and his legs crossed, Anatole Briffaud, known as the Lizard, tossed away the butt of his cigarette, the last drags of which he had just exhaled into the air in blue spirals, sluggishly raised himself with an elbow, and took a look around. The park was deserted, and the sun was disappearing below the horizon.

"There goes the last hour of warmth," he exclaimed, "time for me to return."

He got up, brushed himself off with the back of his hand, and with slow steps took the path from the Boulevard de la Villette.

He was a strong, handsome young fellow, the Lizard. Barely eighteen, blond, beardless, and with blue eyes, he had already set more than one girl dreaming, though not one of them could ever boast of having obtained the slightest favour from him. Anatole Briffaud did not have the least fear or disdain for them, he was simply lazy. The pleasures of love which he spurned terrified him, as did exhaustion. He was horrified by movement. Orphaned at a young age, he had been raised by his sister, Big Ernestine, a streetwalker of no great reputation from the Boulevard de la Chapelle, whose affection for him had been blind. Ernestine could have been his mother, and she could never get used to seeing anything in this youth other than the little mite she had bounced on her knees. And then, he had been so delicate, so slender, so blond! They had never forced him to go to school, they had never compelled him to take any apprenticeship, and his life had passed until this day in calm, without clouds, with no cares for the morrow other than that of the need to lie down.

Anatole was proud of his sobriquet of "the Lizard," which for him gave a sort of validation to the lifestyle he had chosen. Getting up just in time for breakfast, he passed the summer on the banks of the fortifications or at Buttes-Chaumont, laying with his eyes closed, thinking of nothing.

In the winter he remained indoors, in the corner by the fire or in the back room of a wine merchant's, on the lookout for the slightest ray of the sunlight.

The Boulevard de la Villette was decked out for a carnival. The fairground attractions set up gave their last show of the afternoon. He passed by, dragging his legs, casting a bored look at the displays, full of scorn for those people who bellowed themselves hoarse.

All of a sudden he heard someone call out to him. He turned around and recognised an old friend.

"Hello. What are you doing?"

"Me? I'm going back home, and you?"

"Me, I'm going to get a couple of seats on the carousel. Do you want to take a turn?"

The Lizard gave a gesture of fright.

"You know," the other continued, "that's no fun, we keep up with the carnivals . . . we mess around all the time. It's something you should try."

"That would do me an injury"

"And what have you been doing with yourself . . . since the old days."

"Me, I haven't done anything with myself. I'm always with my sister Ernestine and my brother-in-law Antoine. As I'm not strong they support me . . . they even want me to stick with them. And then besides, my sister earns a good living, so it does for three."

"Want to come and drink a glass?"

"Oh! No . . . I'd be late for dinner. I only have a moment . . . If I don't want to push myself . . . This evening, I'll come shake your hand."

"Until this evening!"

At the Rue Pajol, where he lived, he found his sister in the process of setting the table. He cast himself into a chair, threw his Yokohama hat on the bed and waited.

The meal was uncharacteristically silent. From time to time Big Ernestine exchanged a look with Antoine, a fat rogue of thirty-five years with broad shoulders. The two of them appeared embarrassed, like people upon whom a secret weighs and who dare not speak.

Anatole ate, noticing none of this. The coffee was served without any of the three interlocutors loosening their lips. The Lizard rolled a cigarette and sprawled out on a low couch, according to his habit, in order to aid the workings of his digestion.

Then Ernestine appeared to muster her courage:

"Say then, Totole," she said. "I saw some-one this evening . . . someone who spoke to me about you . . ."

"Ah!" exclaimed the Lizard in a tone of indifference.

"Yes, Marcelle . . . Marcelle Thiziau . . . you know right, the Glass-Eye . . . Would you believe she has just had a disaster . . . her man . . . you know her man . . ."

"The Pole?"

"Yes, the Pole . . . they just sent him down for his last conviction for battery . . . that's sad for her, that! To have been with someone for eight years and to see him taken away to . . . there . . . for nothing. That's the case, they say!"

"If he'd only kept himself calm!" opined the Lizard.

"So," continued Ernestine, "she is now a widow, the poor Marcelle . . . well, do you know what she thought? . . . You know she has known you for a long time . . . she has seen you when you were small. She knows that you are a calm fellow . . . She finds you nice . . ."

The Lizard half rose with a terrified look; Ernestine fell silent and lowered her head. It was necessary for Antoine to intervene:

"Getting to the point," said he in the tone of a serious man who knows how the world works, "you're eighteen years old and not too bad looking. Until now we have cared for you . . . I don't reproach you for it. You're our only family. We owe it to you and we do it out of plain duty, but there comes a time when it's necessary to think of the future. You're of the age to be able to work. At eighteen years old

I was already keeping myself busy . . . I had already made myself a home. You have what it takes to please, and Marcelle has a taste for you. This is a serious girl who has never left her man in need, and if the Pole had always listened to her! . . . And then, she is already of the age where she has a clientele who bring in six francs a day. That's not bad going for the times . . . You have only to say the word!"

The Lizard stood up completely pale.

"So this is your way of getting rid of me?" he exclaimed in a voice strangled with emotion. "Oh, I could never have believed that of you! What do you have against me?"

Then, as Ernestine and Antoine fell silent:

"I see it clearly," he continued, "you want me dead . . . look at me, do I have the strength to work! . . . If our poor mother were still here!"

He collapsed in the chair, annihilated, tears in his eyes.

"Our mother!" cried Ernestine, running over to him, "why?"

"Yes, our mother . . . don't you remember what you have told me so often, about when she died and made you swear to take care of me? Ah! Straight away, at the first opportunity . . . you lie in wait to shove me at the first-comer . . . Look, honestly, do I have the strength to work, me! Look at me compared to Anatole! If you only knew how I feel when I have to do anything . . ."

"You suffer . . . and you say nothing?"

"Of course I suffer! I sweat from nothing more than going to the Buttes. I'll be lucky to live another three years, and not just snap in two!"

"He's right," said Ernestine convinced, "he's too weak. You'll tell Marcelle that she shouldn't count on this."

"Then it's settled!" said Antoine, going over to him, "if you're exhausted, Anatole, maybe you should go to bed?"

"No, I need some air," said the Lizard, who remembered the arranged meeting with his friend, "I'm going out but don't worry, I'll return later. Thank you, you're good comrades!"

And in the evening, as he sat at a table with his friend before a bowl of warm wine, the other boasted to him of the joys of fairground life and urged him strongly to do as he did:

"There's no point in insisting," said the Lizard with great sincerity. "My constitution is just too weak, I'd do myself in . . . As for proof that is true, well, only this evening, I turned down six francs a day!"

DECADENCE

For Rachilde

THE VAUDEVILLE theatre slowly filled up.

In a box dandies in red cravats crowded around the banker, who, with a lorgnette to his eye, explored the far corners of the other boxes.

"Not again!" he said as he reseated himself. "But he will come! I tell you he will come!"

"Nonsense! Impossible!"

"I do beg your pardon! This evening," said Foussard, stressing the words as he spoke, "while taking an absinthe, I met Arsène Meunier there, next door, at the Américain. You understand, I wanted to know where I stood after his break with Mary Staub. Ah well! He responded: 'That's done! Finished! reached its end! A hanger-on, my dear sir! And I will be seated this evening for the show at the Vaudeville with my new conquest, Jane Normand.'"

"Jane Normand! Mary Staub's enemy."

"Exactly. And tonight both of them will come with us to celebrate Christmas Eve at Margeurite Mill's house."

"But finally, yes or no—was Mary Staub Meunier's mistress?"

"By God! At bottom she adores him! Say then! There's going to be a pretty scandal when, in the middle of the scene, she sees them, Meunier and Jane Normand, together. Awkward, for the little Staub!"

Evidently interested, Pierre Le Rozay came over to them. He took the lorgnette from Foussard's hand and in turn passed his wandering gaze over the almost full theatre.

"And besides," continued the banker addressing those of his friends who had just interrogated him, "if you want to be sure about Mary Staub's case, ask Le Rozay, who is in on the secrets of the gods."

"Me!" said Le Rozay, smiling faintly. "Me! No, I assure you, I know nothing at all about it."

"You secretive fellow, go on!"

In this moment three bells rang and the curtain rose on the first act of *The Rastaquouères*.

The piece was by Le Rozay.

It was a realist drama, the bold verisimilitude of which had terrified the critics, but as good sense had, on this occasion, got the better of prejudices, in spite of the denouncements and cabals, a great success had just established the talent of the author and of the lead performer, Mary Staub.

Pierre Le Rozay was a truly cool customer. A dedicated worker, desirous of success above all, he spent his time pruning from his life all that could lead him astray from the goal he had assigned himself. They knew of not one mistress of his.

For him, everything was material for study; in addition, though young, he had achieved a very profound and very precise knowledge of the human heart.

From the first he had divined a great artist in the little Mary Staub. He had taken her on upon her exit from the Conservatoire, following a rather resounding failure, unmerited in his opinion, and pushed her on the director of the Vaudeville.

Her development of the role of the "Shrimp" in in *The Rastaquouères* was a true triumph.

Pierre Le Rozay was as proud of having discovered Mary Staub as he was of having written the piece.

An intimacy had soon united the actress and the author. But the psychologist found himself at a loss.

That kid was a real sphinx! Behind her attractive, little bright face a temperament which defied all analysis was hidden. Pretty, no, but desirable. Her blonde curls, very beautiful, framed a pale face from out of which shone two malicious eyes.

With this came eighteen years and a reputation for wisdom.

Pierre Le Rozzay had seen in this last factor the cause of his protégée's lack of success, but his insight stopped there. Superior women who do not explain themselves have a gift for exciting hatred. By her indifference and her impassibility Mary Staub had already made numerous enemies.

Amongst the curious who did not forgive her for success it was necessary to count a former classmate, Jane Normand, for whom a first prize in tragedy had opened the doors of the Comédie Française. This one had been the delight of many people at first, but after being suddenly crowned a great artist, had settled down. She had stuck from then on to a Russian prince and millionaire. Her fidelity had become proverbial; were it not for her past she would have rivalled Mary Staub.

Her prestige, however, soon subsided, and her mediocre debut at the Comédie Française had turned the public's gaze away from her.

Mary Staub having taken the victory with her recent performance, Jane Normand found amongst her former admirers certain unscrupulous comrades who applied themselves to tearing down the budding reputation of her rival.

They made malevolent allusions. They held forth on the tastes of Mary Staub, on her habit of dressing like a man, of affecting masculine mannerisms, of stealing out on jaunts with her male friends, demanding that they treat her like a comrade-in-arms.

What they forgave least of all was her retinue. They saw her each day parading in merry company with her little air of a precious and depraved boy, at balls, in the restaurants at night, and never had any of those who accompanied her been heard to boast of sleeping with her. This was indecent.

Then insinuations had been set loose perfidiously. Doubts had been cast on her sex; they had spoken of a congenital deformity, a malady.

The clan of the envious was augmented, made way for, by all the old friends of Mary Staub, who, having forgotten at the moment that she was and only wanted to be a boy, had blackballed her mercilessly.

"I cannot retain friends for more than two months," said the actress with melancholy. "I don't know what they get in their heads; it always happens the moment they forget that I am not a woman. It's intolerable."

And in public Mary Staub gave readings of the letters she received, miming the declarations therein. They pardoned the injuries, sometimes, never having been shown as ridiculous even by a woman—above all by a woman.

But, one day, absolutely confounding these malicious gossips, there had come a sudden and serious affair between the actress and Arsène Meunier, the elegant reporter from the *Rabelais.*

Arsène Meunier was celebrated for his good fortune; he specialised in fashionable actresses. The wit that he sowed haphazard throughout his articles was almost as much a source of envy within the Press as his sarcastic humour. He had the flaws of his virtues. With an incomparable smugness he abused his beautiful bearing and illustrious disillusionment, which had left him seemingly impassable, to augment his fame with the reputation of a man dear to women.

And then it was that he had been abruptly ripped from his recent conquests and snapped up by Mary Staub. They were no longer seen without one another, but contrary to habit, on this occasion he kept an absolute reserve. He, who so freely opened the double doors of his bedchamber, never let slip a word on the nature of his new liaison. He became as secretive as the actress.

Then public opinion shifted.

"Meunier had vices; Staub held him by them."

This lasted for several months.

One evening, without giving a reason, Arsène Meunier announced his break with Mary Staub and his union with Jane Normand, the penitent, who, on a nod of the head from him, had dropped her Russian millionaire.

Behind the journalist's reticence they divined a drama, of which no one knew the secret, but which had the gift of exciting curiosity to the highest degree. What then had happened?

As for the indecipherable Mary Staub, was she going to accept the defection of the first man to whom she had accorded her favours? With what eye would she witness, facing her, flaunting himself in the box, her lover of yesterday, this executioner of hearts that she had known how to master, and at his side Jane Normand, publicly taking her revenge?

Moreover, the first act of *The Rastaquouères* was going to end.

In the middle of the general attention Mary Staub launched a rendition when, in the box to the left, Arsène Meunier and Jane Normand appeared. When the silence, broken for a moment by the noise of the little benches, the crash of door loudly closing, the swish of silk and the whispering of the initiates, was re-established, the newcomers fixed their lorgnettes on the Shrimp.

Mary Staub did not flinch and the performance continued its course.

Arsène Meunier was not yet thirty years of age; tall, vigorous, beardless, with a Bourbon nose, he knew how to imprint on his physiognomy an expression of absolute disdain for all things. He accompanied his words with slow, careless gestures. What threw off and irritated his interlocutors most of all was the eternal doubt in which he left them. They never knew for sure if Arsène Meunier spoke seriously without mocking them.

His attitude of a blasé Don Jaun pleased women most of all.

Thence came his successes, about which he affected not to care. Of his life he made a comedy, which he concluded by remaining the dupe. It was very sincerely that he responded in a weary manner: "What's the point?" to the most direct invitations from his mistresses.

Mary Staub had been the very first to take the credit for making him forget his role. He had been astonished to find beneath this envelope of feminine flesh a being stronger than himself.

With Jane Normand, a voluptuous blonde, plump and appetising, but woman to the tip of her finger nails, he had regained his old aplomb.

"Very strong, the little one," cried Foussard, when the curtain fell. "She hasn't flinched. What insolence, this Meunier!"

Then, perceiving that the reporter was watching him, he gave a friendly gesture with his hand.

"Ah, let's see," he continued reverting to his favourite theme, "Le Rozay, do tell me, Mary Staub—has she slept with Meunier?"

"One never knows," replied Le Rozay nonchalantly.

"In any case, this blasted Jane Norman is damnably stupid for dropping her Russian for him."

"Has she dropped him?"

"Damn it, my dear sir, if she hadn't, she wouldn't be here tonight. When one shows up like that one has nothing more to lose."

"My God, one is not compromised by being seen in a box with a friend!"

"And to be seen with an acquaintance like Arsène Meunier, in such Bacchic environments?"

"That depends," responded Le Rozay. "No one denies that Meunier is a dangerous case . . . other than platonically. Besides, where are these Bacchic environments?"

"Tonight, on Christmas Eve . . . at Marguerite Mill's home. You'll see them, since you are invited too."

"Ah! They're going there?"

"Yes! When Marguerite Mill proposed her list of guests to me she insisted so vigorously on having them that I could not refuse, to my regret, moreover." added Foussard, who appeared a little uneasy about seeing the reporter from the *Rabelais* interfere in his private life.

Foussard, a well-known banker from the Chaussée d'Antin, was Marguerite Mill's lover.

At that moment someone knocked on the door of the box.

It was the stage manager.

"Monsieur Le Rozay?"

"What is it?"

"Mademoiselle Mary Staub is having a crisis of nerves. She has broken, has smashed everything in the dressing room . . . She is in a terrible state and refuses to come back on stage

". . . And then, there is no one to replace her . . . only you can pull us out of this ugly mess."

"There it is!" exclaimed Foussard. "She slept with Meunier!"

Le Rozay did not respond. He left the box and followed the stage manager.

In the wings, everything was prepared for the second act; decors, actors and props. They only awaited the three bells.

In the corridor leading to the actresses' room Le Rozay found the dresser.

"Ah! monsieur, you've arrived just in time! There's no way of making her listen to reason! I don't know what has come over her all of a sudden! She just slammed the door on the director and forbid me to open it to anyone"

"Always open it!"

"But my orders!"

"Open it!"

Fearfully, the stage manager put the key in the lock and concealed himself for fear of a new outburst.

Mary Staub, still in costume from the first act, her hair loose, her eyes flashing, was sprawled out on her chaise longue, her head leaning on her left hand. On the ground lay cosmetics and the fragments of a broken make-up case.

"Ah! It's you!" she exclaimed on seeing the author enter.

Without responding Pierre Le Rozay closed the door, sat down on a chair and lit a cigarette

"Really," he said, "I believed you to be stronger. The illusion is slipping now. You love him then?"

"What do you want to talk about?" she demanded, sitting up a little and clenching her teeth.

Le Rozay shrugged his shoulders.

"Don't play about with me. Did you sleep with him?"

"With the man who . . . Ah! No! What do you take me for?"

And Mary Staub flung herself angrily back onto the chaise longue.

"Then, it's quite grave!" shot back Le Rozay, still serious. "My poor friend, you are well and truly a woman. I believed you to be more elegantly vicious, more coldly perverse, incapable of all sentiment. And here I discover in you all the weaknesses of your sex, for you have a sex! So much the worse, it's a shame!" finished the young man with a gesture of disappointment.

"You don't understand this, do you? Why did he come here today? . . . baiting me . . . with that Jane Normand, that vulture! . . . "

"Jealousy, now! Ah! Mary! Decidedly you are not strong!"

Someone struck on the panel of the dressing room.

"Monsieur, they are getting impatient in the theatre, they are tapping their feet. What shall we do?"

"An announcement!" responded Le Rozay. "Announce that Mary Staub has taken a fall whilst leaving the scene and we were required to give her aid, but in spite of her sufferings she will continue to perform, in consequence she begs their indulgence."

"But no! No! I don't want to! I will not perform!" cried Mary Staub.

"Do it," continued Le Rozay, dismissing the stage manager, who hesitated. "Now, get yourself dressed!"

"But I cannot feel the eyes of that woman fixed on me! I am capable of throwing anything that falls into my hand at her head!"

"No! You shall throw nothing! You shall swear to perform admirably and that will be your revenge. Dress yourself, you will thank me tomorrow!"

Brought under control by this calm, this coldness, which contrasted with her exasperation, Mary Staub commenced her make-up for the second act.

"Two or three months ago, as far as I know," began Le Rozay, "you were struck by his glib tongue, by his verve as a journalist, intrigued by his reserves of consumptive cynicism. He amused you, this fellow. Without really knowing why you loved him."

Mary Staub made a violent gesture of denigration.

"Hush! Like all the others there was nothing funny about this. He found it novel to pay court to you. He said to himself that there might be great pleasure in being your first lover, all the more since you seemed to him rather strange in appearance and tastes. He could not grasp you, though. You fooled each other mutually . . . the day he wanted to . . . conclude things . . . when he reached the region . . . you awoke and in your turn did with him . . . as you did with the others."

"Who told you that?" said the actress as she came and stood in front of Pierre Le Rozay.

"You are foolish! Dress yourself now! He left you furious, he threw you over for Jane Normand, your enemy, your very beautiful enemy—she is really very nice, this woman—and you see well that he has judged you accurately, since he wants to make you jealous and that he has succeeded . . . they have triumphed, the both of them . . . you are here, vanquished . . . sullied . . . not daring even to scandalise the ends of their lorgnettes."

"Then what should I do?" demanded the actress.

"Take your revenge, by God!"

"How?"

"First of all, perform! Do what I told you! I will take care of the rest, but perform as you have never performed before!"

"Don't worry! You will see! But then?"

"That is my concern!"

"Monsieur," said the stage manager coming in for the second time, "there's no way of holding them. Despite the announcement, impatience has conquered them all. There is an infernal din!"

"Sound the three bells! Mademoiselle is ready!"

A few minutes afterwards Mary Staub, slightly pale, appeared on stage and was greeted by lengthy applause.

"Well?" asked Foussard on seeing Pierre Le Rozay re-enter.

"That was nothing. Poor Mary was struck by fright. A harmless fall . . . "

"But the stage-manager said . . . "

"The stage-manager doesn't know what he said . . . tell me though, on that note, will you permit me to take Mary Staub to Marguerite Mill's home tonight?"

"But Meunier and Jane Normand will be there."

"So much the better! That will be even more amusing," replied Le Rozay tranquilly.

Leon Foussard opened his eyes wide.

"There must be something going on here," he said, nodding his head.

"No . . . No . . . by the way, Mary will be dressed as a man. You shan't mind?"

"Not at all! Quite the contrary, but I fear it won't go off without some extraordinary antics."

The conversation was interrupted by applause. Roused to admiration, the entire theatre was giving Mary Staub a standing ovation.

Never before, in her stunning role of the Shrimp, had the actress shown such surety at the same time as such ardour.

Called back three times, she returned very calm, a little haughty, and bowed before the public with a cold smile, without even deigning to cast a glance of disdain at the box on the left.

"Well, as for that," said Foussard as he left Le Rozay, "you know, she has been very good, but here, so very good, better than on the opening night!"

"You will tell her yourself," replied the author.

"Is that it?" asked Mary Staub, when Pierre Le Rozay found her in the dressing room in the process of putting her cloths back on.

"Yes! You have begun to win back my esteem."

The hysterical fury of a short while ago, the over-excitement caused by the deployment of all her forces, had left no trace of weariness on the face of the actress.

With the help of her dresser she put her town clothes back on in silence and then, when she was ready:

"What are we going to do?"

"After the curtain rises, the big show! We are going to dine at Marguerite Mill's home with Meunier and Jane Normand."

"Very well," said Mary, whose lips had paled slightly, "and then?"

"I have no order to give you. I have promised you the chance of vengeance, of a public vengeance. Here it is! Only, it will be necessary to dress as a man."

"Let's go! You shall be happy, my little one!"

Followed by the author, she got into a cab and had it drive them to her home on the Boulevard Haussmann.

"Madame," said Pierre Le Rozay bowing deeply before Marguerite Mill, "I have the honour of presenting to you my brother, a student at the Lycée Louis-le-Grand."

Mary Staub kissed the lady of the house's hand courteously.

"I thank you Madam for the honour that you do me."

Silence reigned in the large salon where already around twenty guests gathered, standing in groups and conferring in hushed voices.

All present recognised Mary Staub.

They glanced surreptitiously at the corner where Arsène Meunier and Jane Norman were seated. Before Mary's calmness the two of them felt ill at ease; they were upset with that devil Foussard for not having informed them of this.

With an unshakable aplomb, the actress, a monocle to her eye, made a circuit of the room. She sought out the faces of friends and shook all the hands held out to her, the glass was soon broken. Then, pretending to notice the journalist from the *Rabelais* for the first time:

"The renowned Meunier is here! How are you doing, my dear sir?"

"Oh, quite well, thank you," said the other, slightly ill at ease.

"And my dear Jane, I am so happy you could be here!"

She sat down beside her causally, took her hand and congratulated her on her entry into the "Maison de Moliere." She put such sweetness into her ironic complements that Jane did not know how to react.

"You are very lucky," she added, reverting back to her role of a man, "knowing how to hitch your chariot to a wandering heart like M. Meunier! Oh, you women, what sirens you are!"

And with the mischievous gesture of a depraved schoolboy she kissed a little further up the arm of her neighbour, as Arsène, utterly furious, moved back and laughed drily.

Mary Staub was piquant with her little ruffled look, her full head of hair imprisoned under a blonde wig, curly, perfectly fitted, her form slender and her chest flat. Her black eyes shone amidst her pale face and her thin lips, slightly flushed, let one glimpse a thin band of ivory.

Jane Normand formed a contrast with her, a disadvantageous one for the most part. The healthy appearance of this beautiful woman with her plump body, her flesh on display, drew the eye less than the elegant and sickly grace of Mary Staub.

The aplomb which this latter showed, her nonchalance in men's clothing, her cool cajoleries to a woman who that very same night had wanted to taunt her, unnerved Jane Normand. She was shaken, fascinated.

The actress's fresh lips had burnt her; her restless mind struggled with contradictory ideas. The rivalries of past years, the jealousy of yesterday, the revenge of the evening, all that melted down into a synthesis dominated by the smiling impassibility of this enemy whom nothing could upset, in whom she now found a lover. Beneath the tailed coat which fitted tightly around a body which had the svelteness of an ephebe, on which no protrusion rose to disturb the harmonious straightness, Jane Normand refused to recognise Mary Staub. When, forcing herself to make the effort, she recalled the past; when closing or turning her eyes away, ashamed of her failure, she evoked the old quarrels, she was taken by a rage that left her feeling weak and powerless, a rage immediately quashed by a look, by a word from this enigmatic boy.

An insouciant madness lit Mary Staub's flashing eyes. It seemed that nothing existed for her but the pleasure of the present moment. Now it was official court she paid to her rival. The compliments she launched at her remained without echo. Jane felt no will to revolt or acquiesce. Caressed by her rival's voice, she felt shivers run over her skin, it was as if she had the desire to fall into the arms of this child.

The voice of the head waiter announcing "Dinner is served" broke this tension.

Marguerite Mill rose and took Le Rozay's arm.

Arsène Meunier broke away from the group with which he was chatting and hurried up to Jane Normand, but Mary Staub had already taken the arm of his companion.

"Too late, my dear sir," she said, adjusting her monocle and leading them towards the dining room; "my poor friend," she added with intention, "you always take them too early or too late!"

An insult was on the tip of the journalist's tongue.

"I am going to offer you a serious competition this evening, executioner of hearts! Today, I am a man."

"A small, young man," Meunier corrected.

"If you like; we will soon see."

On the dining table stood a gigantic Christmas tree with the name of each guest hanging from the branches near the cutlery.

Mary Staub, treated as a woman and placed between two men, complained.

She wished to be close to Jane Normand.

They thought it amusing to grant her request.

Marguerite Mill placed Arsène Meunier to her right and, very merrily, the dinner commenced.

Marguerite Mill, one of the last gracious demi-mondes, made house with the honours worthy of a great lady. Although already somewhat marked by age she had such charm that one immediately forgot the faint wrinkles which announced themselves at the corners of her eyes, so amusing and so amiable that one preferred her to most of the insufferable young girls with their idiotic beauty and pretentiousness. Besides, her immaculate throat and celebrated shoulders redeemed all that age could dishonour.

It was still an honour to have Marguerite Mill for a mistress; Foussard knew it and paid dearly for this glory.

Pierre Le Rozay, ever taciturn, looked on with his beautiful aloofness. He embarrassed Arsène Meunier with his piercing, ironic gaze. The journalist knew that Mary Staub had been brought along by the author of *The Rastaquouères*; and that all that he had seen and heard over the course of the hour and which struck him as so curious, so unexpected, that he could only attribute its invention to Le Rozay. He understood that Mary Staub acted with a definite goal, to avenge herself probably, but in what fashion? He wracked his brains endeavouring to foresee and anticipate the blow they were going to aim at him; but neither in the over-exuberant gaiety of the actress nor on the face of Pierre Le Rozay could he divine the truth.

Moreover, the journey from the saloon to the dining room had brought a diversion and allowed the embarrassment and worry of the initial meeting to disappear.

Already, from iced carafes, the sommeliers were pouring infusions of Champagne.

Arsène Meunier and Jane Normand completely recovered their sang-froid.

"By virtue of my power of discretion," declared Marguerite Mill, standing up, "I hereby authorise all! Christmas Eve and carnival are those two privileged dates on which reason may declare itself madness. It is recommended to be extravagant!"

"Where and when must one stop? Are outrages against good manners to be tolerated?" asked Arsène Meunier.

"One can go up to the attempt . . . exclusively."

"But if they have consented?" asked Mary Staub.

"From the instant there is an accord between two wills," replied Marguerite Mill, "it is no longer an attempt."

"Thanks."

And Mary Staub poured her neighbour a large glass of Champagne.

"Ah, you! Why do you ask that question my dear friend," demanded Foussard, addressing himself to Mary Staub, whose lips curled in a smile.

"That is my secret."

"Doubtlessly Mary Staub has the intention of carrying out some regrettable enormity on one of us?" observed Arsène Meunier adjusting his monocle.

"Not on you in any case!" shot back the actress. "Besides, here I am a man and I don't feel," she added casting her gaze around the room, "any taste for men."

"A love between women? Oh!"

"What would you know about that, anyway?" said Mary Staub sitting up and casting a glance at Arsène Meunier.

"Yes, yes! What does he know?" cried the neighbouring guests, who the turn of the conversation amused infinitely.

Le Rozay intervened in the debate.

"My dear sir," said he, "yes, you there against the wall, you owe us an explanation, a lecture on the sex of Mary Staub."

"I recuse myself," responded Arsène Meunier, with the air of a man who knows a great deal but wishes to say nothing.

"For what reason?" asked Mary Staub insistently.

Arsène Meunier felt taken. He experienced a burst of frankness.

"For incompetence."

"I pray the distinguished audience to takes note of this declaration. Until further notice, since Monsieur Meunier does not wish to enlighten you on . . . the delicate point which occupies you, you will permit me to be a man here . . . and in consequence to make, to the very nice Jane Normand, a courtship without which my conduct could take on a malign and disagreeable interpretations . . . for her!"

"But it will be necessary to know, should there be any doubt, if Jane Normand is open to this . . . " observed Arsène Meunier, looking to regain ground.

"I was forgetting that you are Jane's knight. My God! She will choose. To us two, Monsieur Meunier!"

"Bravo, Mary!" cried Marguerite Mill, "my bet is on you!"

Jane Norman had not said a word during this entire scene. She looked at Mary Staub with a kind of fright, taken aback by such aplomb.

But when, in the face of such an audience, she saw herself thrown like a prize-stake between these two antagonists, one of whom was her intimate enemy, a blush spread across her face; she was aware of her inferiority.

Her feminine pride revolted.

When Mary Staub tried to kiss her on the shoulder, she pushed her away with the gesture of an offended queen.

"It seems to me," she said in a dry tone, "that you might have asked, and, for a man, my dear friend, you are lacking in gallantry."

"Bravo!" tossed in Arsène Meunier.

Mary Staub, a little pale, crossed her arms and fixed her neighbour with a smile of disdain.

"In gallantry? How so?" she asked slowly.

Everyone fell silent.

For a moment the two women looked at each other, trembling.

The situation was tense; a diversion was needed; it favoured Mary Staub.

She reverted to the pert tone with which she had made her fortune in the role of the Shrimp.

"Worry not Mary of Neuburg! See! We are not in France!"

And she burst into laughter so genuine, that everyone, even Jane, let it pass.

"It was only a joke."

Only Arsène Meunier was not fooled. He noticed clearly that Mary Staub had not abandoned her idea and how Jane Normand, overcome once more by the general good humour, laughed more strongly than everyone else.

"But the bet goes to me!" he declared

"And me too, by God!" cried Mary Staub, "and whilst we wait let us drink!" And she knocked her glass against that of her neighbour.

The dinner continued and they spoke of other things.

Intoxicated by the lights, by the wine and by the white shoulders of the ladies, the guests grew merry.

In the midst of the mounting drunkenness Le Rozay remained silent.

From time to time, he exchanged a look with Mary Staub, who without forgetting herself for an instant, continued her role of the lover.

Arsène Meunier, for whom the evening had started badly, grew sour with wine. Recovering his journalistic verve, now and again he fired off some perfidious epigram, but he spared Mary Staub. The tacit complicity of Pierre Le Rozay disturbed him visibly. He had too much pride in the affair to leave.

Yet, whilst discussing a celebrated case in which a woman had attacked her lover with vitriol, he declared that the right and absolute duty of the man was to drop his mistress from the moment she refused the fantasies of her lover.

He fixed his monocle on Mary Staub as he said this.

Foussard, already heavily inebriated, made an unfortunate remark. He knew the allusion and, at the moment when all eyes turned towards the actress, exclaimed:

"Caught!"

Mary Staub started. She went pale.

"No one has dropped me," she declared. "I have not had a lover. If one loves me, so much the worse! Because they can die of it . . . sometimes! There have been several examples," she added. "There will be still more!"

This phrase of the actress momentarily threw cold water over the group. They suddenly remembered how the son of a banker had killed himself over her.

"Then, so much the worse for Jane!" uttered Foussard, his voice thick.

In point of fact, Jane Normand, her eyes languishing, no longer seemed to pay attention to what was being said.

Supported by the arms of Mary Staub, her cheeks red, she leaned her head against the actress's shoulder.

"You are very nice," she said, "I love you!"

Marguerite Mill clapped her hands.

"I have won, Arsène, and you have lost!"

And as everyone rose to pass into the drawing room, Meunier went to offer his arm to Jane Normand.

"Choose!" said Mary Staub as she separated them.

"It is you I want," replied Jane and in front of the enraged journalist she moved towards the door, leaning nonchalantly on the Shrimp.

An unseen orchestra began a waltz. The two women embraced and mixed with the dancing couples who were already spinning around the adjoining rooms.

Jane Normand was drunk. She emptied her Champagne glass continually refilled by Mary Staub. Then, forgetting her role, the setting in which she found herself, the events which had brought her here, her feminine instinct awakened. A perverseness pushed her closer and closer towards this boy, a moment ago so impertinent, who between two glasses of frothing Aÿ, had spent every moment imprinting on her throat a kiss capable of making her entire being tremble.

She found those little fascinating eyes so pretty, as she did those thin lips and small white teeth. . . She shivered on contact with that slender little hand with its cool touch and pointed nails.

"This is fun!" she said at first.

Then, warming to the game, an unconscious desire was born within her, which soon rose to the level of a need.

This woman, who loved men for men, was smitten with the androgyne.

Now the waltz with its dizzying whirls had maddened her. Her frustrated flesh revolted. She threw her arms around Mary Staub's slender body with violence.

"I have never seen you like this. You are very lovely as a man! . . . I assure you . . . I would really love . . . I want a lover like you . . . if you were a boy!"

Mary Staub, slightly flushed, laughed.

Suddenly, Jane Normand gave in.

"I cannot do this anymore!" and she let herself fall onto a sofa. "Come here Mary!"

"You will be better after taking a turn. The waltz has exhausted you. Let's go and see what they are doing elsewhere!"

Arm in arm, holding on to each other, the two woman left the ballroom. On the threshold of an anti-chamber they encountered Pierre Le Rozay.

"Come!" exclaimed Mary Staub in a low voice as they passed.

The author gave a little nod of the head.

He lit a cigarette from one of the chandlers and followed the two actresses from a distance.

They walked softly through the series of rooms, caressed in passing by the stroking leaves of the great exotic plants which made a hot-house of the apartment.

All of a sudden they disappeared behind a curtain.

When in his turn Le Rozay gently opened the door, he stopped, astonished.

The two women were in Marguerite Mill's boudoir. Only candles lit the chamber hung with red satin.

Mary Staub was sat on a sofa, and stretched across her knees was Jane Normand.

With a quick movement, this latter had torn back the shoulder straps that held up her bodice; her skirt was spread out as her blonde curls fell in golden cascades over her shoulders.

Her nostrils dilated, she implored with both look and voice.

"I love you, I want you, hold me, take me!"

Mary Staub pursed her lips; she crossed her arms and considered her defeated enemy with a malevolent smile.

"How vulgar you are, how like a woman. For you, with you, all it takes it a glass of Champagne to make you do all sorts of stupidities! But you don't see that, do you? But what do you want me to do with you, my poor girl?"

"Whatever you please!"

"Whatever I please! . . . But you still haven't noticed that I only wanted to mock you? Why should I take you? You're a whore, my dear friend, and me, I'm a virgin!"

"Virgin!" exclaimed Jane, half sitting up, "Good! So much the better! Take me, tell me, do with me as you wish! I cannot say anything else to you . . . I love, I want you! Order me! I will obey you!"

She clutched Mary Staub's slender body, but that other remained motionless, her eyes mocking.

Le Rozay approached slowly, very near. He sat down on a love-seat and watched.

"What do you say, Pierre, do you want her? That would be amusing."

Tranquilly, Le Rozay made a gesture of refusal.

"What a whore!" declared the Shrimp with disgust, and stood up brusquely, letting Jane Normand fall.

She got up, seized Mary Staub anew in her arms, and inclined her lips towards her mouth. Blood rose to Mary's face; in her turn the sexless ephebe felt drunk on the woman's scent. Her eyes blazed. At last, sadistically, she bit Jane's lips and then her neck to the point of drawing blood, and then she opened wide the large door which gave onto the ballroom, and pushed her victim brutally into the midst of the surprised dancers. Drunk, dishevelled, her lips bloody, her corsage ripped open, Jane fell straight into Arsène's arms.

"I'm returning her to you, this mistress of yours!" shouted Mary. "You can go sleep with her, if you fancy."

And she closed the door again with a crash.

Mary Staub fell to the sofa, exhausted. The effort had been too much. Her entire body was gripped by a nervous spasm; her teeth ground together, her delicate fingernails tore at the satin of the divan.

Pierre Le Rozay, very calm, stood close to the fireplace considering her.

A great silence reigned; at last the actresses' nerves relaxed themselves, she lay back, unable to do more, and her eyes turned towards Le Rozay, she smiled and held out her arms.

The writer remained unmoving.

Then Mary stood up; rapidly she crossed the room and opened the door:

"Decidedly the cleverest men are sometimes imbeciles"

"Is that directed at me?" asked Le Rozay curiously.

"Maybe!"

She went out.

Le Rozay followed her slowly.

He found her in the antechamber, putting on her fur coat.

"You are leaving?"

"Yes."

"Good, let's go!"

In the coach Le Rozay did not stop smoking. Mary Staub, leaning in the corner, uttered not a word.

All of a sudden the vehicle stopped on the Bolevard Haussmann.

Mary Staub was home; she climbed down and waited on the pavement, the door open.

"Give my address to the coachman!" demanded Le Rozay.

"So you . . . "

"What?"

"Ah well! One could say that you are pretty strong! . . . strong in a different way to me! So much the worse! No hard feelings?"

"You're a fool!"

And the two of them shook hands.

IN EXTREMIS

I.

ONE evening, as she was in her dressing room changing her costume between the second and third acts, Lucy Peyrannes was suddenly struck by the look of sadness on the face of Mère Verteuil, her lady's maid, a good creature who always had a cheerful word ready, and who had often comforted her in her moments of boredom or exhaustion. The woman's face looked drawn and her eyelids were red.

"What's the matter? What has happened to you?" asked the actress, and the other answered:

"Ah, Madame, I am in great trouble; my husband is a house-painter, and yesterday he fell from the top of a ladder. His leg is broken, and he is in the hospital."

"Pooh!" cried Lucy gaily, "a leg fracture is not a serious matter; he will not die of it, mark my word. Cheer up now, and I will go and see your husband myself, tomorrow."

"Oh, thank you, Madame, that will please him so!"

II.

Lucy Peyrannes was celebrated in artistic circles for her unconquerable cold-heartedness, upon which indeed she prided herself. Though not beautiful, she was the possessor of a fatal fascination, and had often been loved madly. One man had killed himself on her account, and if any one mentioned that catastrophe she would give a little pout of disdain as she said:

"How can you blame me? I cannot reciprocate every one's sentiments, I was not made so. It is not my fault! In the city as on stage; if I am a harpy, I cannot do anything about it."

And in fact she owed to three such roles the most beautiful success of her career.

III.

The following day, at noon, she arrived with her lady's maid at Lariboisiere Hospital. En route she stopped to buy out a fruiterer. As she spread out peaches, grapes and other delicacies upon the sick man's bed, she said, merrily:

"These will help to pass the time, Père Verteuil. So don't go saying we don't take care of you."

The old man looked confused and stammered:

"Oh, Madame, you are good, too good, but it is too much for me!"

And then he added in a low voice:

"Give a few of these delicacies to my right-hand neighbour. Poor boy, no one comes to see him, and he has not very long to live."

Lucy turned, and in the next bed lay a beardless man of perhaps twenty-four, but whom sickness had given the look of a child. He was gazing at her with dark brilliant eyes which seemed to contain all the life that was left to him.

His thin hands, as pale as wax, were spread upon the counterpane.

Lucy felt moved by the gaze of the dying man. She hesitated for a moment.

"He is dying of consumption," continued Père Verteuil.

Then Lucy approached him.

"Would you like to have a peach and some grapes?"

"Oh yes, Madame," he whispered, and a look of unutterable joy lighted his face, while his hands moved feebly.

"Then do me the pleasure of accepting these," said Lucy, laying a fine bunch of grapes before him. "You have been ill a long time, I suppose."

"Yes," he answered, and then as if her tender sympathy had woken in him strength not felt for months, he added, "and you are the only one who has shown any care for me for a moment. Thank you, thank you."

Two tears rolled down his pale cheeks, and his hand clasped hers as he tried to raise it to his lips.

Lucy, for what may have been the first time in her life, felt moved; she experienced a sudden surge of tenderness for this poor, forsaken being who was going to leave this world without having felt any other joy, for all she knew, than that which she had just given him.

"You have no relation, no friends?" she asked.

In a weak tone, hardly above a breath, and interrupted repeatedly by fits of coughing, he told her his story. He had always been delicate, and unfortunate; his mother had died at his birth, and his father married again, he had been driven from the paternal house, though only twelve years old, to take care of himself. Since then he had tried many ways of earning his bread, but had been without help, without friends, and when his health gave out he was forced to come to the hospital for shelter.

He was condemned, dying, he knew that, and was not sorry, for he would be at rest. In a few days perhaps, his corpse would be wrapped up in the sheet he was lying on, and carried down to the dissecting room. He did not fear death, but he would have liked to have lived a little before dying. What had he ever done to deserve such a miserable existence? Every Thursday and Sunday the other patients had friends come to visit them, and knowing that others cared for them they could bear their suffering more easily, but no one ever spoke to him, him whom nobody had ever held . . .

A sob cut off his words.

"Listen," said Lucy, whispering in his ear after a moment's silence, "every Friday and every Sunday, I will come to see you, would you like that? I too have no-one to love . . . Well, I shall be your little mother!"

The young man could not speak, but she felt his right hand clutch hers.

Then she leant over him, pressed a kiss upon the dying man's brow, and hurried away.

IV.

"I do not know what you did to my neighbour," said Verteuil the next time Lucy came to see him, a few days later, "but he is a great deal stronger. He has talked of you all the time, and has counted the days and hours since you were here. This morning he was able to sit up, to wash and dress himself, and comb his hair. My word, he has a good colour—just look at him."

And, in fact, the invalid's cheeks were almost rosy. His dark humid eyes were fixed, with a look of grateful tenderness, upon the lady, "the good lady who loved him so."

Lucy sat down beside him with her arms full of dainties, complimenting him upon his improved looks, and whispering a thousand pretty fancies in his ear.

"This makes me want to live," he said. "I am so happy now, that I cannot bear to die."

"You are not going to die, my dear, but to get well," she answered gaily.

"So . . . I had seen others here. . . like me! They always got better . . . the night of their death."

But Lucy did not tire of her role of sister of mercy, and, during the weeks that followed, she came at two o'clock every Friday and Sunday to her little friend's bed.

V.

One evening she arrived at the theatre still dressed in the garments of mourning, her eyes red.

They had buried the little one at four o'clock, and she had followed him to the cemetery.

Every month she goes and lays a wreath of flowers upon the grave she had raised for him.

And now, when any one reproaches her for her hard-heartedness and indifference, she answers:

"Like all people, I was born capable of loving, but I spent my whole wealth of affection at once . . . So you cannot therefore expect me to give any more!"

Printed in the USA
CPSIA information can be obtained
at www.ICGtesting.com
LVHW040354220124
769411LV00104B/1107